BRAIN DEAD GORGEOUS

BETTER OFF FED
BOOK 1

STUART WAKEFIELD

write-hearted books

For the hopeful, the hungry, and the heartbroken. You're not alone.

CHAPTER ONE
THE ARRIVAL

IT WAS the kind of January grey that seeps into your skull and whispers, "today's not your day."

First day of Spring term—yes, *Spring*—and the early morning sky sagged like a wet towel, and through it all oozed the school playground smell of mildew, teenage hormones, and Lynx Africa.

I stood under the bike shelter outside B block, coatless, naturally. If you wore a coat at my school, you'd get called something ending in "-boy". Instead, I'd perfected the Year 13 uniform of cultivated resistance. Blazer slung over one shoulder? Check. One shoelace untied? Affirmative. One eyebrow permanently raised? We have liftoff.

Scattered across the drizzled tarmac, groups of kids clung together like bacteria, developing in their little social petri dishes. The footie lads were already kicking a soaked, scuffed ball across the concrete, laughing like the law of being miserable in British weather didn't apply to them. A few rebellious Year

11s loitered under the bike shelter opposite, vape clouds curling like Tim Burton mist. Huddled in a doorway, someone was playing tinny grime out of a phone cradled in their hoodie.

I was as ever, unaffiliated. Holly, my best (read: only) friend, hadn't rocked up yet. No doubt she'd have some outlandish excuse when she finally arrived.

"Some Jehovah's Witnesses wedged a stack of salvation under our front door and jammed it shut."

"A bus stop advert for oat milk triggered me and I had to sit down about it."

"My cat staged a protest on my shoes. Proper sit-in. Tiny placard and everything."

The other kids didn't dislike me exactly. It was just that over the years I'd become one of the extras who fill up corridor space in a teen movie. The boy teachers forget halfway through registration, and whose name is always said with a question mark.

Spoke too soon. Holly was ambling across the playground towards me, rocking the frizziest hair since her infamous hundred metre sprint at last year's sports day, and with the biggest pair of head-phones I'd ever seen slung around her neck.

She fist-bumped me. "All right, you poof?"

"All right, you slag?"

"Crap night's sleep," she said, rubbing her generous belly.

"You on the blob?"

Kissing the back of her teeth, she elbowed me in the ribs. "Not everything's about periods."

She adjusted the waistband of her skirt, a little self-conscious. Lately she'd been dropping hints about wanting to look "different" by summer, but this was the first time she'd looked genuinely uncomfortable in her own skin.

"We're at school," I said. "It's all about periods."

Holly didn't reply, so something had to be wrong.

"Seriously, though. You okay?"

"Remember that girl off TikTok I told you about? The skinny one?"

I looked to the sky and squinted in mock memory recall. "Can you be more specific?"

"This one," Holly said, shoving her phone in my face to show me a girl indistinguishable from every other influencer.

"Looks like she hasn't blinked since COVID."

"She's got this new diet thing out."

What this had to do with Holly not sleeping, I'd no idea.

"And...?"

"I bought some, and it's, you know..."

Ah, the belly rubbing.

"Given you trapped wind?"

She dropped her voice to a whisper. "It's very much *not* trapped."

How do I not laugh?

"You didn't sleep because you were farting? Like, all night?"

"Keep your voice down," she said. "Doors have ears."

"No, walls have ears. *Walls.* And keep your

farting down. The last thing I need is you guffing all the way through the Biology practical."

"Thanks for that, gay boy. Still, I lost two pounds overnight. Probably water weight, you know, from the… wind."

Mansplaining mode engaged. "While flatus—"

"What's fla—?"

"—is produced in the digestive tract, which is moist, the moisture in the digestive system is not significantly transferred into expelled gas."

Her face went blank. "Hang on. Did you say we've got a Biology practical?"

"Duh, it's mocks week."

In less than a second, her hands covered her face. "I thought it was mocks next week. I've only revised a bit."

I gave her a tentative sniff. "And you only whiff a bit."

She practically folded in on herself. "I might have bought the diet thing and added that diet thing to another diet thing."

I narrowed my eyes. "What other thing?"

"Cabbage soup."

"Cabbage soup?"

"My gran said it was all the rage in her day, and you know how skinny people were in the First World War."

"Jesus. How old's your gran?"

"Okay, maybe the Second World War."

"So, let me get this straight. You've turned your gran's cabbage-water weight loss soup into a TikTok fusion diet?"

"That's not the point, Jack. The point is that I'm finally losing weight."

"Hey," I said, putting an arm around her shoulders, "that's great. You'll probably fail Biology, but at least you'll be able to pull off a crop top."

"You're such a shit. I just... you know... want a boyfriend."

I gave her a quick peck on the cheek. "You and me both, babe."

Holly elbowed me and nodded towards a rotten bench. "Remember when I had that crush on Amit?"

Amit sat cross-legged, hoodie sleeves chewed to threads, hunched over his laptop like any self-respecting geek. He looked up just long enough to clock me and give me the kind of nod you'd give someone you've never actually spoken to but somehow know exists. I nodded back, two ghosts acknowledging each other.

"You liked him," I said, "because he gave you his last Fruit Winder in Year 7."

Holly clutched her chest as if it were a tragic romance. "Sacrificing his strawberry and apple for me? That was basically a proposal."

"You also said you liked the way he smelled of cheese strings."

"Shut up," she said, but she was smiling.

And then, because fate is never subtle, *he* arrived.

I felt it before I saw it—that ripple in the social fabric. A hush started in the far corner of the playground and moved like a tremor across the tarmac.

Conversations clipped themselves short. A football skittered to a stop. One of the Year 11s paused mid-vape like she was buffering. Even the phone's owner cut the tinny grime track dead.

A black Range Rover glided to a halt as if it was auditioning for a car commercial. Chrome trim, tinted windows. I half-expected a fog machine to go off. The passenger side door opened, and out he stepped: tall, lithe, and smug enough to make the Cheshire Cat look miserable by comparison.

The inky, architectural miracle of his hair shone even in the absence of sunlight, not a strand out of place. It was the kind of hair that costs eighty quid a trim and comes with a complimentary smirk. Shirt crisp, tie loose in that deliberate, I-couldn't-care-less way that takes effort and at least three mirror checks. His brogues gleamed as if he'd buffed them with unicorn spit, and his leather satchel was tastefully aged. For a fraction of a second, his expression faltered, like he'd been holding his breath before stepping out. It was gone quickly, buried under the smirk, but it was there.

When did Tom Holland start doing his GCSEs?

He didn't just walk; he *arrived*. His strides were confident without being cocky, like he'd rehearsed this moment but wanted you to think he hadn't. The wind caught the hem of his blazer at just the right moment. Somewhere, a seagull cried reverently.

"New kid," someone murmured behind me, which felt a bit like saying, "Water's wet."

My lips curled before I could stop them. The

classic reflex of pretend-you're-too-smart-to-be-impressed-so-no-one-notices-that-you-absolutely-are. I scoffed, low and sarcastic. Despite myself, I'd already filed away the hair, the walk, and the precise angle of his jaw.

He didn't need to look around. Everyone had already rearranged themselves around him like he was centre stage, and I was in the front row, trying not to clap.

Around him, the spell took hold.

A group of Year 9 girls burst into giggles so high-pitched they could've shattered glass. The footie lads started over-kicking the ball with sudden, wild ambition. One nearly decapitated a Year 7. Even the school prefects, gods of aloofness, shifted their weight and actually *looked*.

I started drafting a list in my mind. One, hair like a shampoo commercial gone to a whole other level. Two, smile engineered to make parents trust him and girls spiral. Three, school uniform tailored within an inch of its life… and half an inch of his pecs.

Naturally, I told myself it was research, not admiration. Definitely not fascination. More like the way a zoologist observes a lion, or a fire warden notes the location of the nearest extinguisher.

Miss Doyle emerged from Block B like she'd been summoned by pheromones. Clipboard in hand, her eyes twinkled in a way they definitely hadn't twinkled when she gave me detention last term for "breathing with attitude."

"Ah, you must be Greg!" she said, beaming.

Her voice pitched up like someone had squeezed it. The vowels stretched and softened. Her entire face did this... thing, like she was smiling at royalty or a surprise puppy.

Greg, of course, returned serve with charm. I didn't catch his exact words—something polite and perfectly pitched, no doubt—but the effect spread like cologne. Girls leaned in, lads scowled slightly less than before, and even the caretaker paused on his way to fix whatever toilet was today's toxic hazard.

Greg was assigned to 13C. My form. Because of course he was.

Ahead of us, he followed Miss Doyle down the hall with the ease of someone walking into their own party. There was no hesitation, no checking for signs. He just moved with terrifying, awful grace, like he already belonged. Like the school had been waiting for him.

I slid into my usual seat without ceremony, back row and one from the wall. Greg ended up two rows from the back and third from the wall. Close enough to track and far enough to ignore if I wanted to. Which I didn't.

He adjusted his tie. Miss Doyle made a delighted note on her clipboard. I stared very hard at the scuff on my desk and tried not to wonder how long it would take for him to become a bonus prefect, steal the title of Head Boy, or be voted Prime Minister.

He'd barely sat down, and already the room felt smaller.

I added to the list. Four, smells like wealth and almonds. Five, sits with a casual elegance that suggests his bones are editorially trained. Six, laughs like a warm knife through buttered insecurity.

Every time he spoke, the room recalibrated. People sat up, heads nodding. Even Miss Doyle started framing her sentences like an improv partner: "Yes, and…" It wasn't that he was liked. It was that his presence made you question whether you were.

And me? I clung to fascinated resentment like it was SPF in a heatwave. I couldn't afford to be earnest, not around someone like Greg, so I told myself it was academic. A study in social manipulation. A cautionary tale. The problem was that very time he smiled, I felt the list mutate, and that terrified me more than I let on.

By the end of term, Greg had infiltrated the football team, drama club, debating society and, I shit you not, the school band.

He played the accordion. *With sincerity.*

You'd think that would've tanked his mystique. Instead, it raised him to Taylor Swift levels of folklore.

"He's so quirky."

"He's talented and humble."

"My mum saw him at Waitrose and said he's got the X factor."

It was like watching someone speed run popularity.

Sometimes, though, I caught him watching the room too closely, like he was checking to see if the spell was still holding. The charm never slipped, but the way he scanned faces told me he needed the reaction as much as we gave it.

He could answer a question wrong in Physics and get praised for "thinking outside the box," whereas I once got a stern look for "blinking too aggressively" during assembly. Every corridor became a catwalk. Someone said his handwriting was "aspirational". A teacher once offered him a cup of tea. Like, *from the staffroom.*

He laughed easily, moved confidently, and carried his damned leather satchel like it had chosen him in a wand shop.

At some point, someone created a TikTok compilation of his candid moments, except you could tell he knew when people were papping him. Every pose looked lifted from a cologne ad. 'Eau de Effortless.'

Meanwhile, I remained exactly where I'd always been: background noise with a pulse. Except now, the background was getting blurry, because I wasn't just watching anymore. I was *tracking.*

Two months after Greg rocked up, I was watching a Snickers bar cling to its vending machine coil like it owed me rent. My last quid was gone, and still no chocolate. It was just me and the quiet humiliation of being outwitted by a snack dispenser.

"All right, Jack?"

The voice came in low and easy, like it hadn't just detonated my frontal lobe.

Greg, Ribena carton in hand, smile soft, and his eyes lazy in a way that says, *I don't try, I just exist.*

I made a noise like I was reeling off my pronouns. "Er. Yeah. You?"

He nodded once, cool and detached, then walked off, vanishing into a sea of admirers like some teenage Gatsby. The entire exchange lasted maybe three seconds. Four, tops.

I, however, relived it for hours. Said it to the mirror that night. "All right, Jack?" Tried it with different inflections. Was it curious? Friendly? Flirty? Habitual? Had he meant to say it to me? Had he thought I was someone else? Wait, was there another Jack at school…?

The next morning, I saw him in the corridor. He didn't say a word. Didn't even glance in my direction.

By lunchtime, I'd started a full psychological investigation.

New list. One, had he said my name, or had I imagined it? Two, had there been an actual smile? Three, what did Ribena mean in this context?

I told myself it was absurd to care. That it was a blip. That he probably said, "All right?" to everyone, except he hadn't said it to everyone. He'd said it to *me.*

A few days after that, he waved at me in the car park. The day after, nothing. In Art, he passed me a glue stick with a grin that bordered on conspiratorial.

A couple of days later, in Geography, I muttered something about erosion that wasn't meant for anyone's ears. Greg chuckled. Actually chuckled, like he'd been listening. I looked up, startled. He caught my eye, and I nearly passed out from the adrenaline spike. Then he immediately looked past me, like I wasn't worth the breath it took to laugh. By the end of the lesson, he'd gone back to ignoring me.

It was like being ghosted in real time.

I'd moved on from list-making to cataloging everything. Column A, date and time. Column B, context of interaction. Column C, body language. Column D, level of eye contact.

I gave up pretending it was a character study anymore. It was a case file.

The inconsistency was the killer. If he'd just been a twat, I could've filed him under 'Emotionally Hazardous, Do Not Touch' and moved on.

Was I imagining his interest? Probably. Did that stop me? Not a chance. And you know why? Because it's not the grand gestures that ruin you. It's the little almosts. The maybe-smiles. The fleeting kindnesses. The scraps. A hand brushing yours by accident. A smile that lasts a beat too long. A word spoken softer than it needed to be. None of it enough to prove anything, but too much to ignore.

Greg Beauchamp was a master of leaving scraps.

He'd also become the baseline, the bar, the golden calibration against which the teachers quietly measured the rest of us.

"Perhaps take a leaf out of Greg's book."

"If only you applied yourself like Greg."

"Greg's essay is an excellent standard to aim for."

There's a specific kind of invisibility that stings. Not being ignored, but being noticed only in contrast.

The interaction cataloging stopped. Instead, I found myself clocking the exact time he opened his locker (08:27), the flavour of crisps he preferred (prawn cocktail), and how he always sat nearest the window if he had the choice.

I'd started sketching him from memory. Not in a romantic way, but studies. You know, like you'd sketch a Roman bust to prove you could.

Even the library betrayed me. Greg got extended borrowing rights from Ms Mulgrew, who double-checked *my* returns like I was a known page-ripper.

The ecosystem had shifted, and I was still trying to breathe the old air.

The rings came next. One silver, subtle band on his pinky, and another on his middle finger. Boys at our school didn't wear jewellery. Jewellery was for girls. Needless to say, Greg's rings didn't raise eyebrows.

Not that anyone would question His Right Royal Greg Beauchamp. He could wear jewellery, write poetry in the margins of his books, cry during a film in assembly, and no one would think twice. Greg was obviously, unshakably straight. The kind of straight no one second-guessed. He could have quoted *Clueless* word for word and no one would have batted an eyelid.

He got to be expressive without consequences. *I* didn't.

I'd been 'known' since Year 8. Not officially and

certainly not in a celebratory TikTok caption kind of way. In my school, I'd been whispered about, side-eyed, then boxed up and unremembered.

Greg got admiration from the staff. *I* got warnings. *Greg* wore softness like a cardigan. *I* was told to toughen up. *He* was theatrical and cool. *I* was dramatic and attention-seeking.

Still, I watched. Hope is a sponge. It soaks up every glance, every maybe-smile, every scrap. Hope for what, though? To be chosen by Greg? By anyone?

CHAPTER TWO
CABBAGE SOUP AND CARPET DEPRESSION

THE DOORBELL RANG in that specific rhythm that heralded Holly: impatient, unapologetic, and just short of smashing it in.

I opened the door and there she was. Hair freshly braided, white faux fur coat already sliding off her shoulders, and a suitcase bulging with, I assumed, the existential dread of prom dresses.

"You look like a prossie."

If I'd had been anyone else, she would have head-butted me.

"Your house smells like carpet depression," she said, stepping inside. "Got glasses or are we drinking straight from the bottle tonight?"

She hoisted a bottle of what claimed to be rosé but looked like melted bubblegum. Her smile looked sharp enough to cut, but the shadows under her eyes gave her away.

"Classy," I said, leading her to the living room.

"Excuse me, but this was on offer and also

supports local British sugar dependency." She flopped onto the sofa. "I brought those weird prawn cocktail crisps you suddenly like."

"I've always liked prawn cocktail crisps."

"Yeah, and I've always liked watching *Mamma Mia!* while chewing gravel."

We sat in the glow of my mum's aggressively beige lamps, knees almost touching. The TV was on but muted. Some dating show where everyone looked like they'd been printed off the same glossy template. Mum was nowhere to be seen.

Holly cracked the bottle and took a long swig. "So," she said, already grinning, "how's your emotional hate-boner for Greg?"

I groaned and pulled a cushion over my face. "Dead, deceased, cremated."

"Liar."

"He said 'Hi' to me yesterday."

Her eyebrows shot up. "And?"

"And today he walked past me like I was a traffic cone."

"A traffic cone," she said, nodding like a sage, "with unresolved yearning."

"He's infuriating, like charisma was cologne and he bathed in it. And it's not even real charm. It's... I don't know... *weaponised*. It's like he's some sort of Bond villain but with better skincare."

"And yet still you know his entire timetable."

"Coincidence." I sniffed the air. "Wait, you're still on that soup thing? You must be two stone down already, and it's barely March."

She nodded, reaching into her coat and pulling out her bright pink Stanley cup. "Twenty-eight pounds down and it's all down to cabbage, green tea, and—" Her hand trembled slightly as she popped the lid. For half a second, her grin faltered, like she wasn't sure whether she was showing me soup or the thing that was slowly swallowing her.

I eyed it. "You're still buying that TikTok diet stuff? Do you even know what's in it?"

She took a sip with theatrical pleasure. "Who cares? I'll be glowing at prom."

"You'll be glowing because your guts are fermenting."

Holly paused just for a flicker of a moment, her eyes red around the edges. Not in a mascara-run way, but like she'd pulled an all-nighter crying into a radiator.

"You okay?" I asked, quieter now.

A blink, then it passed.

"Fine," she said. "I'm still detoxing. My body's basically a temple under renovation."

"'Detox' is code for starving."

"No, it's code for 'aesthetic reset.'"

"Same thing, really. Just shinier branding." I wanted to tell Holly that starving yourself wasn't a glow-up; it was slow self-erasure, but jokes were easier.

We let the silence stretch. The TV kept flickering muted snogging. Somewhere upstairs, the boiler made its usual death rattle.

For a second, I wanted to say I hated that she felt

like this. That I got it, that the pressure chewed people up and spat them out skinny. Instead, I smirked and said, "You'll vanish completely, and then I'll finally win an argument."

Holly curled her feet beneath her. "Seriously though. Are you gonna come to prom or not?"

I made a noncommittal sound and picked at a sofa thread like it held answers. "It's months away."

"Because I'm not going without you, Jack. It'll be tragic. Like *Strictly Come Couples Therapy* tragic."

"I'll think about it."

She leaned her head on my shoulder. "Think faster. Time waits for no queer."

A moment passed, then she barrelled into the kitchen, cheeks flushed, her enormous cup clutched in one hand and her suitcase in the other. Her energy filled the room like a cheap perfume: intense, cloying, and oddly exhilarating.

I hurried after her. "You okay?"

"Of course, dear boy, but I have things to show you. *Wonderful* things."

Taking a seat at the kitchen table, I lifted one eyebrow in the lazy, practiced way I'd perfected after years of watching emotionally constipated male leads in period dramas. "You arrived like the trailer for a disaster film."

"And I'll be a box office smash." She beamed, practically vibrating. "You should see my arms. No bingo wings, Jack. *None*. Look."

She shoved one arm in my face, flexing like a pageant contestant who'd just discovered deltoids.

I leaned back, unimpressed. "You're seventeen. Seventeen-year-olds don't get bingo wings."

"Details, details," she said with a wave of her hand. "Sixty-six more pounds and I'll have the boys fawning over me."

"Sixty-six? That'll make you…" I did some basic maths. "Ninety-ish pounds. You're basically ingesting boiled sadness and hoping to vanish."

"It's *not* boiled sadness."

"I'm assuming this influencer didn't run their diet thing past the Food Standards Agency."

"No need when it's *this* elite. *This* cutting edge." She swung her suitcase onto the counter and offered me the oversized cup. "One whiff, instant enlightenment."

"I'd rather snort bleach."

She rolled her eyes but laughed, plonking herself down opposite me. The cup let out a faint hiss as she twisted open the lid and steam spiralled up, carrying a scent that was indeed boiled cabbage but with a sharp chemical edge. Something sour-sweet like a soiled nappy masquerading as cinnamon.

Gran's old cabbage soup on its own might've just made her fart through double Maths, but Holly had spiked it with someone's magic powder. Retro diet meets TikTok detox. An unholy alliance.

"Doesn't it smell divine?" she cooed.

Gagging, I waved the flask away. "Smells like something my mum would pour down a blocked drain."

"I'll take that as jealousy," Holly said brightly,

taking a long, dramatic gulp. "I've been documenting my cabbage weight loss hack online and now I have—"

"Nearly seven-hundred-thousand followers."

You told me a dozen times already.

Her eyes were wide. Too wide. Her pupils looked strange, too. Big, watery black pools, like she'd mainlined espresso.

"I'm making a killing as an authorised reseller of Carmen's—"

"Carmen?"

"Keep up, Jack. The girl from TikTok I showed you. She's the genius who started it all. When she shared my cabbage soup hack, my followers doubled overnight. Half the girls at school have bought from me, *and* a few boys." Her skin had that over-exfoliated sheen, and she started blinking like her lashes were ticking off a countdown.

I opened my mouth to ask if she was okay, but she'd already launched into a monologue about hem lengths and the exact logistics of sneaking a vape into her clutch on prom night. Yes, she was too much, but somehow something felt wrong.

"Come on, try some," she said, thrusting the cup under my nose. "It's earthy, but in a gourmet cleanse kind of way. It literally flushes your system."

"I like my system unflushed," I said, recoiling, "and organs that still trust me."

Clearly delighted by her own dietary bravery, she laughed. "Cabbage is the new kale, apparently."

"Was kale ever the old kale?"

"Don't be thick. This stuff works. Look at my collarbones."

Yanking down the neck of her top, she revealed her clavicle, which looked, well, like a clavicle. Slightly protruding and definitely nothing I hadn't seen before, but she acted like she'd just revealed a new planet.

"You're glowing," I said flatly, "albeit radioactively."

She laughed again, louder this time, and I noticed it carried a tinge of hysteria. Her hands drummed the table in a rhythm too fast for casual fidgeting, and one of her pupils had dilated.

I frowned. "You sure the stuff you're taking's safe?"

"Totally. The website's got, like, ten thousand reviews. All five stars."

"From verified humans?"

Eyes rolling, she started yanking swathes of fabric out of her suitcase. "You're just bitter that I'm going to look hot and you're going to turn up, assuming you do turn up, in some funeral suit looking like you're attending your own breakdown."

Despite myself, I smirked. "Accurate."

Holly's fingers twitched again, reaching for her cup with too much urgency, then she took another gulp, sighing as if it was the purple potion from *Death Becomes Her*. "Honestly, this soup's changed everything. I've been feeling so alive lately. Focused, energised, ready to seize the—"

"Day?"

"Night. *Prom* night." Her eyes glittered with an intensity that didn't sit right. There was excitement there, also something forced, something unnatural. A mania hid just beneath a high-functioning break-down or, worse, beneath something unfamiliar.

"No side effects?" I asked.

"No… Well, one. You know those binaural beats I used to listen to when I was revising? Can't stand them now. Makes me feel like my insides are twisting."

"That's weird. Have you tried ASMR instead?"

She shot me a disapproving look. "Cranial nerve exams get on my cranial nerves."

The back door creaked open and in shuffled Mum, carrying a paper-wrapped bundle that smelled like heart disease and joy. She dropped it onto the counter like a bag of evidence, peeled back the paper, and revealed her dinner: a mountain of chips glistening with oil, battered cod the size of a brick and, somehow, the most despondent mushy peas I'd ever seen.

"Evening, Holly," she said, plucking a chip without looking. "Still trying to turn prom into the second coming of Christ?"

Holly wrinkled her nose, eyeing the chips like a starving Victorian urchin. "Mrs Harwood," she said, "I'm on a cleanse. No solids after six."

"No solids after six weeks of starving, got it."

Holly glared at Mum. "My diet's metabolic science."

"So's rigor mortis."

I snorted.

Holly faked a laugh and reached for her cup again, perhaps as punishment. "This," she said, waving it like a sommelier, "is how you prepare for a major event. Discipline and commitment. *Greens.*"

Mum studied her for a moment, then slowly separated two chips that had fused together. "Back in my day, school discos were warm orange squash, a questionable DJ, and a strobe light if you were lucky. All the embarrassment, none of the fun."

"That's because your generation had no ambition," Holly replied, her tone airy but eyes a touch too sharp.

"Ambition," Mum said, biting into a chip. "Is that what it's called when you spend the best part of five months starving yourself to impress some halfwit boy in a hired suit?"

Holly froze, the soup halfway to her lips.

I sucked in a breath. "Mum…"

Mum huffed. "I'm just saying that all this fortified cabbage nonsense won't end well. Slow dances don't go well with explosive diarrhoea."

"It's not just cabbage," Holly snapped, recovering. "It's a detoxifying metabolic reset."

"Oh, well then."

Holly's eyes lingered on Mum a moment too long, narrowed like she was filing the insult away. When she smiled again, it looked pasted on, the kind you wear for cameras.

I watched the exchange unfold with quiet admiration. Mum rarely engaged with anything more taxing than an ITV drama, but now and then, she slipped into this dry, vaguely philosophical mode where everything sounded like it should be carved into a pub wall.

She was already halfway through the cod fillet when she looked at me and said, "You going to this thing, then? Prom?"

Holly gasped as if Mum had insulted the monarchy. "Of course he is. Tell her you're going."

I cracked my neck. "Wouldn't miss it."

"Bold," Mum said. "If I were you, I'd stay home and watch telly. Less risk of being emotionally eviscerated."

"You're such a ray of sunshine," I said.

She shrugged. "Runs in the family."

There was a pause just long enough for Holly to re-assert control of the room.

"Well, I think it's going to be amazing," she said. "Everyone's going to be there. They might even crown Greg Prom King. Can you imagine?" Her eyes sparkled.

For the first time, I saw it, the real reason for her persevering with the soup, the frantic energy, the forced glow. She'd started starving herself for a boy, but now she was starving herself for one particular boy.

And the worst thing? I understood. Still, understanding didn't blunt the jealousy that was doing all kinds of shabby things to my stomach.

· · ·

Fifteen minutes later, Holly had transformed the living room into her personal catwalk.

Mum had retreated to her armchair fortress and turned the volume of both the TV and her indifference up to twenty. I sat slumped on the sofa, watching Holly, draped in fabric, twirl in the centre of the room like a fairy-tale princess reared on social media and casual teenage trauma.

"What do you think?" she asked, striking a pose that was half *Vogue*, half clumsy toddler. "Bear in mind that I still have another four-and-a-half stone to lose, maybe five, so this is a proof of concept."

The fabric, pale pink, ruched in a way that screamed Pinterest board, hung off her with unsettling ease. It did, I had to admit, show off her collarbones, her narrowing waist, and her feral commitment to perfection.

"You look like an aggressive cupcake."

She practically shone. "You are the perfect gay best friend." A second spin, faster this time, and the fabric flared around her knees like a bell. "This is my year, Jack. Everyone will remember me." The way she said it didn't sound like hope. It sounded like a threat to the universe itself, as if memory could be forced into people by sheer willpower. "You feel it, right? That weird vibe in the air? Like we're on the cusp of something massive."

"Possibly food poisoning."

Ignoring me, she plopped down beside me on the sofa, snatching up her cup like a trophy. "I mean it. Something's already started."

"You're lightheaded from malnutrition."

"No." She shook her head a little too fast. "It's more than that. I feel buzzing, like every cell in my body is vibrating with—" She stopped suddenly, her face tightening.

"What?" I asked.

She screwed her eyes shut. "Headache. Behind the eyes. Still detoxing."

"That'll be your witch's brew."

Giving me a tight smile, she drank deep, the sound thick and wet.

"At the rate you're going, you're going to turn into a cabbage."

Her laugh had a strange kind of delay, a fractional moment before it kicked in, then she stood again, suddenly restless. "I need heels," she said, hurrying towards her suitcase. "The silver ones. No, gold. Gold's better. Gold's *regal*."

Her limbs jittered like a marionette pulled by invisible strings. Her face gleamed with sweat, her pulse fluttering wildly in her throat, but she kept smiling, kept planning, kept talking about who might be Prom King, whether Greg would come alone, whether her dress would make "that bitch Ava Waterson" spontaneously combust from jealousy. She was spinning a dream with manic precision, every stitch sewn in hunger and something else I didn't have a name for.

It felt like she was vibrating at a frequency the rest of us couldn't hear.

• • •

An hour later, the front door slammed behind Holly with the usual flourish, followed by the aggressive revving of her Volkswagen Polo as it peeled off into the night.

"What's she trying to do?" Mum called from her chair. "Outrun common sense?"

I wandered back into the kitchen to find the dreaded Stanley cup sitting on the counter. Picking it up, I debated whether to throw it directly in the bin or just bury it under a tea towel and pretend I hadn't seen it. Instead, I twisted the cap off. A slick ribbon of steam escaped, winding into my nostrils with a vengeance. It smelled worse now. Stronger.

"Christ," I said, tipping the dregs into the sink. The thick green sludge stuck to the basin like it didn't want to leave.

It took a full sink and a hefty squirt of Fairy to get the smell to fade. As I scrubbed, my hands in the water, the remnants of the soup clung to my skin longer than it should've, like it was waiting for something. Some switch I couldn't see.

I turned off the tap, dried my hands, and stood in the growing quiet, the air heavier and closer than I'd ever known it.

Behind me, my mum coughed, muttered something about *NCIS*, and turned the volume up again.

The itch in my gut was nothing. Holly was just being Holly. The soup was just soup, but even after the sink cleared, I swore I could still hear a faint, fizzing note somewhere in the drain, like the soup was humming to itself, waiting.

CHAPTER THREE
CUSTARD CREAMS AND ETHANOL

AT THE END OF JUNE, after weeks of gruelling exams and watching Holly slip away into new circles of friends, I went to prom. Maybe stupidly, I thought if I showed up, I'd still matter to her. For one night, at least.

As much as I wanted to loathe it, I had to admit that the school hall glimmered with the sweaty effort of transformation. Streamers hung from the rafters, party lights looped between the annual school pictures, and a disco ball spun smoothly above, like it was happy to have been invited. The middle-aged DJ was already filling the space with sound that no one danced to. Some EDM remix of a viral hit, the bass-line thudding through the soles of my shoes like a distant threat.

Prom. The great British tradition of the school disco remixed and remodelled to be more like the American teen movies. Somehow, calling it "prom" made it glamorous. The reality was anything but.

No limos, no corsages, no chocolate fountains. Six quid a ticket, and a suspicious bowl of punch that smelled like a six-pack of Red Bull had infiltrated a gallon of antifreeze.

I hovered by the double doors, pretending to look at my phone while I scanned the crowd.

Mum was right. Everyone was trying too hard. Girls in heels they couldn't walk in. Boys in tuxes that didn't fit. Gaggles of tipsy teens shrieking about exam results and who'd snog who later. And then, you guessed it…

Greg.

He stood near the stage, one hand hooked lazily into the pocket of his tailored trousers, the other gesturing mid-story to a circle of enraptured onlookers. He laughed, and the sound carried across the room like music.

He looked *unfair*. Hair shining under the lights, sleeves just tight enough to show off his biceps, eyes gleaming with that dangerous charm he wielded like a blade. Someone handed him a drink. He sipped it, winced theatrically, and the crowd laughed.

I hated him, and I wanted him.

As I walked the perimeter of the room like a ghost at a party for the living, no one stopped me. No one noticed. That was the trick, really. If you don't exist, you become exceptionally good at observing the people who do.

Where the hell's Holly?

Taking up post by the buffet table, right next to a tragic, untouched display of cheese cubes and limp ham sandwiches, I watched as Greg rotated in and out of other conversations, moving and magnetic.

He hadn't seen me, and I told myself that was a good thing even as something in my chest prickled with the heat of relative proximity. Holly was right; tonight *was* different. My problem was that I didn't know whether I was ready for it.

I poured myself half a cup of the punch, immediately regretted it, then pretended to sip as if it wasn't eating the enamel off my teeth.

Across the room, Amit hovered by a stack of chairs, tugging at his tux jacket like he'd only just got it out of the bag, faint lines that hadn't had time to breathe out. Back in the day, he'd had a little puppy fat, but tonight he looked taller and narrower.

If Holly didn't manage to snag Greg tonight, I half-suspected Amit would be her second choice.

Behind me, a couple snogged with the urgency of people about to be airlifted from a war-zone. I turned away and studied the dessert end of the buffet like it held the secrets of the universe. Instead, all I found was a lonely plate of custard creams and an unenthusiastic trifle.

The voice landed in my spine before it reached my ears.

"Living the dream?"

Greg stood there, hands empty, smile idle. *Alone.* He looked like he'd stepped out of a film and into my life with the lighting already adjusted. His bowtie was undone and his shirt unbuttoned just far enough to show the meeting of his pecs. His hair, too perfect to be accidental, swept across one eyebrow in a way that made me momentarily forget how to stand.

"Depends," I said, trying not to choke on my own tongue and gesturing to the custard creams. "Do these count as one of your five-a-day?" My joke wobbled out of me like a baby giraffe taking its first steps. If he noticed, he didn't let on and just smiled in that slow, deliberate way that made me feel both chosen and exposed.

"Keep Year 10 away from the sausage rolls," he said.

"Year 10? But this is our prom."

"Interlopers," he said. "Feral little goblins."

"I'll fend them off with homework."

He stepped closer, just enough to make me feel it, and there was a shift in the air. Cologne, warm and woodsy. His eyes flicked to my cup. "You're brave. That stuff's practically ethanol."

"I'm pre-toxifying."

He laughed.

Ohmygodhereallydoesthinksimfunny.

All around us, the music slowed into a synth number no one knew how to dance to, and for a moment it felt like we were in a snow globe. Two figures trapped in suspended disco ball glitter.

Holly climbed up to the DJ booth like an underweight spin-class coach high on kombucha. In a second, she'd grabbed the mic and instead of saying, "Here's one for all the lovers in the dark," she hoisted her Stanley cup over her head and yelled, "Welcome to the ultimate cleanse. No refunds, but the glow-up is killer!" Her voice cracked on the word killer, too high, too forced, and for one awful moment the crowd went quiet, like they weren't sure whether to laugh or call an ambulance.

All I could do was bury my face in my hands.

"She's had quite the transformation," Greg said, watching her carefully. "There's nothing left of her."

Holly stood like a shadow of a girl trying to remember how to be radiant. Her prom dress, pink silk and strapless, clung to collarbones that jutted like punctuation marks at the ends of her shrugging shoulders, and her cheeks were hollowed, like someone had pressed their thumbs in and never let go. Lip gloss glinted at the corners of a mouth held in a practiced pout, but her eyes kept scanning the crowd like she was searching for someone to notice she didn't belong.

"I hope someone's checking on her," Ava Waterson said to her clique in mock concern. "That's not wellness. That's *withering*."

Ava was right. Holly wasn't glowing; she was collapsing, and the school had all clapped for it, mistaking collapse for transformation. No one had stopped to ask the difference.

Holly's eyes darted to Ava for the briefest second. The smile she wore stayed, but her knuckles whitened around the mic.

Despite the DJ's best efforts to claw his mic back, Holly continued, "And tonight you'll be getting the first play of my bestie Carmen DeVyre's new single!"

What? I'm her bloody bestie.

Guilt twisted in my chest. I'd been so focused on my exams and so fascinated with Greg that I'd let my friendship with Holly wither, too.

"Great," Greg said, watching Holly make a random spectacle of herself. "Another TikTok wannabe singer." He turned to me. "Have you been drinking that cabbage crap?"

I blinked. "What? No, why?"

His smile tilted, sly. "Didn't expect you to look so good." Then he added quickly, "Not that you usually look bad, I just never see you try".

I didn't know what to say to that. My brain lit up like a Christmas tree and then promptly short-circuited. All I managed was a very elegant "Oh."

He gave me an appreciative once-over. "You're really not drinking Holly's soup?"

"God, no. I had a close encounter with the stuff. Clung to my skin like a needy boyfriend."

Chuckling, Greg leaned in. "She tried to get me to have some in double Chemistry. Said she was 'aesthetically reborn' or something."

"Right." I said, brightening at our shared experience of Holly's relentlessness. "I'm staying carb-committed."

"Rebellious," he said, his voice dropping half an octave. "I like that."

My mouth was dry. Or numb. I couldn't tell the difference.

Just then, the DJ started playing some old-school hits. *Lose Control* by Missy Elliott pumped through the speakers, but still he cranked up the volume. The bass thudded in a way that didn't feel like music anymore. It was lower, deeper, like it was vibrating in my teeth.

My forearms prickled, and a nearby group of girls gagged visibly and sprinted for the toilets. But it was Holly who had the biggest reaction. She clutched her stomach as if the sound itself had reached inside her.

What the actual fu — ?

"Want to go somewhere quieter?" Greg's hand twitched at his side, and he swallowed like he'd just shared his deepest secret.

The lights caught his eyes just right.

I stared. "Quieter?"

The impossible moment hung there like a snowflake about to land, fragile and magical. There was no one else within earshot. The music, the lights, the drunken laughter. It all receded to the edges of my mind, like candy floss dissolving in water.

The smile was still there, but it wasn't the grin he gave his adoring fans. This time, it was something smaller and less confident.

I nodded again, this time with more courage. "Yeah. Okay."

He didn't move right away, just tilted his head and looked at me like he was memorising something. Then he walked toward a nondescript door in the corner of the room. I followed—*Holly'll be fine*—legs unsteady as though they'd forgotten how to carry the weight of possibility.

The corridor outside was colder than I expected.

The dim overhead lights hummed, and the smell of disinfectant and old trainers hung in the air.

Trailing a few steps behind Greg, I became hyper-aware of my prickling forearms and how the sensation dulled as we moved farther away from the music.

What if someone noticed us leaving?

Greg didn't speak or even look back. He just kept walking, one hand brushing against the wall as he moved, like he was counting the whitewashed bricks. A poster peeling from the wall read, SEIZE TODAY OR REGRET TOMORROW.

"Where are we—?" I started, but he turned to walk backwards, smiling like he was in a music video.

"Relax," he said when he reached me. "I'm not leading you to your death."

"That's reassuring," I said, trying to sound amused and failing.

At the end of the corridor, he shouldered open a door, and a gust of cool night air slipped through. Glancing back at me, something flickered in his expression. "Come on. I only want to talk."

My heart was a drumbeat in my throat. Given half the chance, I'd do a lot more with him than talk, so I practically sprinted through the door. If this was the day I was supposed to seize, then I'd sure as shit not regret tomorrow.

The night outside felt sharper than it should, like it was waiting for something.

We were behind the school now, tucked in the

narrow service alley that ran between the hall and the drama studio. Everything smelled faintly of damp brick. A row of staff cars sat beneath yellowing security lights, mostly old bangers with National Trust window stickers and overstuffed dashboards.

One particular car stood out like a black panther among stray cats. His parents' sleek Range Rover, polished to mirror perfection.

Greg sauntered over to it, fished the key fob of his trouser pocket, and then unlocked the doors. "Hop in," he said, voice edged with mischief. "It's warmer."

There was a split-second where I saw the whole situation from the outside. A quiet spot in the staff car park, a boy whom I barely knew aside from his glossy exterior, and a car door open like the entrance to a tunnel...

...but then he looked at me and smiled his *bloody attractive smile*, and that was all it took. I slid into the backseat. He was right—it was warm and quiet and (bonus) everything smelled like him: aftershave and clean laundry.

"Budge up." He got in after me, closing the door with an expensively soft thud that sealed us in. The world outside faded instantly, muffled behind tinted windows and leather upholstery.

I sat there rigid, hands in my lap, trying not to breathe too quickly.

Greg stretched his legs out and turned slightly, so he was facing me. "Comfy?"

"As comfy as I've ever been in the presence of mystery and mild terror."

He laughed, low and genuine. "You're weird, Jack."

"It has been said."

He didn't look away, didn't lean back. He stayed there, close enough to touch, close enough for me to count the freckles on the bridge of his nose.

I didn't know what was about to happen, which, for once, wasn't the worst thing in the world. For a while, neither of us said anything, the only sound the muffled bassline escaping from the hall, underpinning the swell of an unfamiliar dance track.

"Must be that TikToker's new track," I said feebly.

Greg drummed his fingers lightly on his knee, then *my* knee, then he moved his hand up my leg.

Mortified, a part of me was swelling right along with that dance track.

"You watch everything," Greg said. "Like you're collecting it."

I blinked, surprised that he'd noticed anything I did. "That sounds ominous."

"I didn't mean it like that. You see things other people miss." He said it without a hint of mockery.

Swallowing, I shifted in my seat. "You've been watching too?"

He didn't answer straightaway. What he gave me was a look that made time slow down and hovered somewhere between confession and challenge. "Perhaps I noticed you before you noticed me."

He's lying.

Still, I let myself believe it for one fragile second.

"You're always… *there*," he added. "Not trying, like the others. Not caring. It's annoying."

"Thanks…?"

"I mean it in a good way. You don't pretend."

I wanted to tell him that people like me didn't get to exist in ambiguity the way he did. That his charm was a currency I'd never have, and his ability to slip between personas made him both dangerous and irresistible.

Instead I said, "Neither do you. You just brand it better."

For a moment I couldn't tell if he wanted to kiss me or catalogue me, and maybe that was the point.

"You're clever." He huffed out a little laugh. "I hate that."

His fingers pressed into my thigh, his thumb moving upwards just a fraction. The world went very, very still, and my throat tightened. As he leaned forward, it was like the whole car was folding in around us, full of breathless anticipation that made your skin feel electric.

My heart knocked against my ribs like it wanted out.

His gaze flicked to my lips.

I let my lips part, just slightly.

Then came the sort of sound you don't notice until it's too late.

CHAPTER FOUR

NOT PRIDE WEEK

ALL AT ONCE, the car windows sank down with a mechanical whir. My head snapped up. Greg's did too. His hand wasn't anywhere near the controls.

A rabble outside howled, phones glowing. He looked as stunned as I felt, caught in the headlights of his own friends. The crowd gathered around the car, phones up and recording.

One of the footie lads dangled a key fob in the air like a trophy. "Smile for Grindr, Jack!".

Each phone was a reminder that this moment wasn't just happening. It was being saved, clipped, maybe already uploaded. The thought made my skin crawl harder than the damned music.

Greg's hand, once resting on my thigh, vanished as if it'd touched fire, then he laughed. Not the soft one from before, the one that made me feel like the universe might have room for people like me. No, this laugh was armour. Fast and loud, and meant for everyone but me.

"Did you really think I wanted to kiss you?" he said, voice twisted into something acidic, burning down every fragile hope I'd been stupid enough to build. For a moment, he looked at me as if he regretted saying it. Like he hadn't meant to, like the words had outrun him. His eyes flickered. Panic? Guilt? But then it was gone, smothered. "Come on, Jack. It's prom, not Pride Week."

The crowd whooped like we were in a sitcom. Phone lights flashed, catching the corner of his handsome bloody face.

I didn't move. I *couldn't* move.

"He actually leaned in," he said to the crowd on his side of the car, loud enough to carry over the jeers. "Eyes closed and everything."

"Proper tragic," someone crowed.

The laughter spiked, sharp and jagged, almost in sync with the beats from the hall. For a second, it felt like the crowd was one organism breathing through the same throat.

My throat closed. My skin burned.

Greg was doing what he always did: staying above it all. Finally, with something that might've been regret flickering beneath his smirk, he said, "Bit of advice. Don't believe in everything you want."

I couldn't survive staying, so I pushed my way out of the car and through the mob.

Everything was louder now. The music and the shrill delight of people who'd witnessed something hilarious. I couldn't feel my legs properly. I couldn't feel *anything* properly. My body moved without input, like a marionette with cut strings still twitching from muscle memory.

Behind me, someone shouted, "Want a ride home, Jack, or just a cry?"

Another wave of jeering. The world blurred as if I were watching it through glass smeared with grease.

Something soft hit my back. Crumpled napkin? Crisp packet? A bit of a sausage roll? It didn't matter. Everything had tilted.

For a moment I looked back.

Greg was still in the car, his face illuminated from within. In his eyes I saw something like shame, sharp and bright, but he looked away before it took shape.

I wanted to scream at him. Ask him *why*, if any of it had been real, but I couldn't bear the sound of his voice again. I walked, then stumbled, then ran. Howling followed me like a tailwind, bright and brutal, echoing in my ears. I didn't know where I was going. Past the bike shelters, through the gap in the fence behind the storage container where people sometimes went to smoke weed, and on into the dark that reeked like damp leaves and bad choices.

A carousel of *ifs* spun in my head. *If* I'd stayed home. *If* he hadn't smiled like that. *If* it hadn't felt real.

Was it real? Even a little?

The look in his eyes said it was. Had he planned it? Had it started one way and ended another because he's a coward? Because he doesn't know who he is when he's not performing?

My insides felt like they'd been scooped out and

filled with lead, like every dream I'd ever allowed myself had been dragged into the light and laughed at until it was crushed. I wanted to cry, to scream, but more than any of that, I wanted to rewind the clock seven minutes. Back to when I thought he wanted me, and I clung onto that thought. That's what hurt the most.

I ended up behind the cricket pavilion, crouched low against the wall, back pressed to the cool wood cladding, lungs dragging in air, hands clenching into fists. Still, they shook. In the silence, I realised it wasn't silence at all. A low hum buzzed at the edge of my hearing, like feedback from a bad speaker. Or maybe it was just the echo of the voices, warped and replaying inside my skull, an echo corrupted by static.

Humiliation burned within me in an infinite loop, and my chest hurt like someone had filled it with something sharp. I'd been stupid. No, worse than stupid. I'd been hopeful.

That's the thing no one warns you about when you're queer and quiet and watching the world from the outside. Sometimes the thing you want most will walk straight toward you, smiling, and you'll reach out, and it'll bite, and still you'll wonder whether its smile was real.

I wiped my face with my sleeve. I'd started crying, but I had the sudden feeling that the tears wanted to be rage, and the rage wanted to be clarity. I wanted to understand him, to know why he did it. I wanted to peel him back layer by layer until I found the part of him that cowered, and then I wanted to examine it.

I pressed my head back against the wall, breathing slowly. The world hadn't ended, but something inside me had died and left something biting behind. It wasn't just heartbreak. It was a splinter lodged under the skin, small but impossible to ignore, already working its way deeper.

CHAPTER FIVE

THE GLOW-UP IS KILLER

IT WAS ALMOST an hour before I returned to prom. I had a loose plan to wait until Greg was crowned Prom King, then climb up on stage and have it out with him. He'd apologise, beg for forgiveness, then confess his love for me to the entirety of Year 13. There'd be applause, subtle at first, that would grow into cheers of overwhelming support. If Greg Beauchamp loved me, then everyone else would fall into line, right?

The image dissolved as quickly as it had come. Even in my head, it felt flimsy, like tinsel strung over a rotting Christmas tree. Something in the air already smelled wrong, though I couldn't place it.

As I approached the school hall, one door was open. Not wide, but enough to let out a sliver of light and noise, but not the *right* noise. The bass-line was still going strong, but over it came this high-pitched screech that wasn't quite feedback and not quite melody. It rose and fell in weird mechanical hiccups and reminded me of that ancient dial-up modem recording Mum once made me listen to, so I'd understand how hard it was for Neanderthals to check their Hotmail.

If Carmen DeVyre thinks she's going viral with this song, then— Wait, why is her song still playing?

The sound wormed its way under my skin, and my forearms prickled again. It wasn't just a noise, though—more like a rhythm that wanted to sync with my brain. Binaural beats gone horribly wrong and a screeching squeezed between them.

Then there was the smell. Not sweat, booze, or teenage hormones. It was something acrid and sharp, like bile and burnt hair. Chemicals reacting to heat they were never meant to touch.

A girl burst through the doorway, her dress soaked in something dark and thick. Her eyes were wild, the whites flashing, and her mouth foamed at the corners. She looked right at me and screamed like a saw blade was tearing through her throat.

I sprang back as she sprinted past, barefoot, clutching her shoes in one hand. She smelled faintly of cabbage and sugar, a sickly sweet tang I knew too well. The scent clung to my throat even after the girl vanished into the night.

From inside the hall, there was the sound of glass shattering, another scream, then a low, wet, animal growl.

I took a breath and crept in.

Okay, okay, so I know what you're thinking. Why

the hell would I go into a school hall that was so obviously auditioning for *Stranger Things*?

Answer? Holly. She was my best friend once, and despite the cabbage soup and Stanley cup sermons, some tiny part of me still thought I owed it to her to check. Plus, I was one of the extras who fill up corridor space in a teen movie, remember? We always snuff it first.

The hall had been transformed again. The disco ball had stopped spinning and hung like an eye popped from its socket. Music still pumped from the speakers, and the screeching was as strong as ever. Couldn't anyone else hear it?

Wait, where is every —?

It was like the screeching had made me blind to the horror that unfolded before me.

Everywhere, people were on the floor, twitching or screaming or silent. A girl in a turquoise dress puked something thick into a struggling boy's mouth. The boy convulsed, eyes rolling back, then he collapsed. Miss Doyle was slumped over the buffet table, shaking so violently the trestle legs thudded in time with her spasms. The music, the screeching, the retching... it all braided together into one relentless soundscape, and the disco lights strobed over it like some sadistic god was filming the worst music video ever made.

Instinctively, I ducked low.

The air was thick with something that smelled like copper, as though someone had microwaved a butcher's bin.

Then I saw Holly.

She stood in the centre of the chaos, feet planted like the eye of a hurricane. Her dress was ripped at a side seam, and her Stanley cup lay crushed at her feet. Her wide eyes, pupils blown white, and irises ringed in crimson met mine. She didn't speak. She just tilted her head and smiled. My Holly wasn't there anymore. This was someone hollowed out and filled with static, her grin stretched too wide, too long.

"Holly?" I darted forward, then I saw what she was holding and self-preservation brought me to a stop.

Ava Waterson's head, ripped clean off her body.

Grunts sounded behind me. One of the drama kids was being pulled to the ground by two others. They buried their faces in his torso, hands gripping him like anchors. He didn't even scream. He just gasped once, then went limp.

My body lurched towards him because somehow my first thought wasn't "escape," it was "help". I didn't think about them attacking me. There wasn't time. My only instinct was deep and stupid and human. I lunged at one of the boys clawing at the drama kid, and tried to wrench him off. My hands slipped with sweat, blood, and something that trembled and thickened in time to the binaural beats. Holly's soup wasn't just soup anymore. Carmen's additive had turned retro dieting into something monstrous.

The boy turned toward me, and I recognised him.

He used to hang around the art block and draw anime girls in his sketchbooks. Now his mouth was covered in blood and his eyes were clouded, milked over like a week-old corpse, but alive somehow. And furious. He hissed, then bit me. One motion, no hesitation, just deep into my shoulder, straight through my tux. The crunch was obscene, like biting into an apple, only I was the apple.

Scorching pain exploded through me. A branding iron pressed straight into the bone. I screamed. At least, I think I did. Everything around me slowed. Blood arced in the air, then the world shrank into the bite, into the wet suction and the teeth grinding through my skin.

I shoved him off, staggering backwards until my legs gave out. The ceiling spun, and I saw Holly one more time. She was laughing loosely, like the string tethering her to reality had snapped.

Everything tipped sideways, and darkness bloomed.

When I woke, the world seemed quieter. Sure, there were sounds, but they felt different now. Duller.

I blinked. The barest hint of moonlight filtered through the windows, grey and watery.

A girl dragged herself towards the doors, but the boy who'd collapsed earlier had his jaw around her foot, biting rhythmically like a metronome.

I should be screaming, thrashing, clawing at the air, but I wasn't. Either the shock had numbed me, or something had climbed into my body and stolen the panic.

I pushed myself up, limbs sluggish, then flexed my fingers. They moved slowly but obediently, despite being—

Why are my hands turning… blue?

Pressing one palm to the slick floor, I pushed myself fully upright.

Across the room, the school pictures were cracked, the glass protecting them veined with fractures. I stumbled toward them, catching my reflection.

The skin beneath my eyes was a deeper blue, and my lips had lost their colour. My hair was plastered to my forehead with sweat, and there was a smear of something across my cheek. The eyes staring back at me were still mine. Bloodshot, yes, tired, yes, but a little milky. Not quite like the whited-out windows I'd seen in the others but close enough.

Tentatively, I touched the wound on my shoulder. It had crusted, dark and angry, but there wasn't any pain.

Why doesn't it hurt?

And there was a faint hum of something underneath my senses, a growing hunger that sat at the back of my mind like an alarm I'd snoozed. Present, insistent, but not overpowering.

A breath caught roughly in my throat, and I said out loud, "Jack". The sound of my name grounded me. I was still here. Changed, yes, but not lost. Whatever this thing was, it hadn't taken me, not completely, which meant I wasn't alive and I wasn't dead. I was something caught in between, teeth already itching for a taste of—

Somewhere in the back of my skull, a word pulsed: *meat*. Not chips, just warm meat.

I could murder a Big Mac.

CHAPTER SIX

NO BREATHEY, NO BITEY

THE DOORS to the main school opened with a reluctant groan. As I stepped into the main corridor, its fluorescent lights buzzed.

What had once been the polished artery of school life was now destruction's wake. Posters flapped uselessly on the walls. EXAMS ARE JUST AROUND THE CORNER! one announced, smudged with something brown. A can of Coke rolled lazily near my foot. Smoke drifted from somewhere, with a metallic sting in the air.

And bodies. God, the bodies. Some lay crumpled in heaps; others were pressed against lockers, necks at unnatural angles. One girl slumped in a chair by the water fountain, head tilted back like she'd dozed off during a revision break, except her chest wasn't moving. No rise and no fall. Empty husk.

My stomach lurched. These weren't just bodies; they were people. People I'd passed in corridors, people who'd moaned about exams, borrowed my pens, scribbled in textbooks, laughed too loud in lessons. Ordinary, annoying, *alive* people.

I should've felt something sharper. Grief. Horror. *Anything.* Instead, there was just a blank. Maybe that was the soup, or maybe that was me.

Whatever had changed me hadn't touched the girl in the chair. She'd just died.

Why? Why her and not me?

The not-knowing scraped worse than the smell.

A girl with a shredded dress limped out of the toilets, dragging one foot. Her jaw hung too low, like it had dislocated in the rush to bite. Her left hand was bent sideways at the wrist, bones protruding like a grotesque corsage. She staggered towards me with the oddest expression.

I froze, held my breath, waiting for another attack, but she moaned once, low and bubbling, and kept going. My pulse skittered.

Then another emerged from the science wing. A teacher, I think, or what was left of one. His jacket hung like torn skin, and his eyes were a fog. He walked straight past me too, like I wasn't there.

Another one came shuffling out of my form room. He didn't acknowledge me.

They weren't ignoring me; they were *accepting* me. Filing me under the same category as themselves.

If I don't breathe, they don't see me?

I shambled (might as well play the part, right?) towards the nearest one, a girl in a dress soaked so fully in blood it looked like dyed satin. Her hands hung limply at her sides, and her jaw opened and closed like a fish, slow and senseless. Holding my breath again, I waved a hand in front of her face. Nothing. Moving even closer, I tapped her forehead with my index finger. Still nothing. If they thought I was one of them, maybe I could walk through hell untouched, or maybe it meant I already belonged here. I swallowed, then stepped deliberately on her foot. A wet sound came from somewhere inside the ruined heel of her shoe, but she didn't even shift her gaze.

I moved back, and she trundled off, the corridor swallowing her.

Yup. No breathey, no bitey.

One of the footie lads, tux torn in half and one arm missing, walked like a wind-up toy someone forgot to turn off. When he was alive, he'd had a stammer and loved anything Marvel. Now he was just a body with the vaguest of directions.

In that strange, liminal space where the undead didn't care about anything but the living, I felt a loneliness sharper than any bite. I wanted to catalogue it, analyse it, but my thoughts were fogged. Maybe that was the point. However the soup and… *signal* worked together, they didn't just twist bodies; they rewired how they felt. The invisibility I'd spent years hating was suddenly the only thing keeping me alive.

Like all the kids, I knew the school's layout by heart. I set off at the same painfully slow speed the zombies had, first making my way through the history block, then up the stairwell with the dodgy handrail where Holly once tripped and broke a rib. The building was a maze of memories now. I shuffled carefully, fear burned into me, not knowing how fragile this invisibility was or how long I had. I'd partly turned, but maybe it was a slower process for me somehow. Maybe it would take me, eventually.

Then voices. Real voices. Not moans or groans or those terrible chewing sounds. I stopped, pressed myself into the alcove outside Lab C, the chemistry room with the rusted fume hood and ancient Bunsen burners.

Through the cracked glass, there were moving shadows. Five or six kids were huddled behind benches, desks barricading the door. One of the boys clutched a hockey stick, and a girl had what looked like a fire extinguisher.

"Holly bit Miss Doyle," one of Ava's friends said in a harsh whisper. "Full Biology practical."

"Pass or fail?" someone muttered automatically.

"Pretty sure 'devoured' is a distinction."

A boy with blood on his sleeve said, "Greg left us. Just ran. Didn't even try to help."

"Don't," another snapped, voice cracking, "don't say that. Maybe he panicked."

"Panicked?" A boy's laugh came sharp and ugly. "He shoved Ava at Holly. That's not panic, that's strategy."

"Did he make it?"

A pause.

"I heard a crash. Near the gym."

The girl hugging the fire extinguisher to her chest whispered, "If he comes back, do we let him in?"

"If anyone comes in here, I'm aiming for his bollocks," a boy growled.

"Or *her* bollocks," someone muttered from the shadows.

"Or *their* bollocks," another shot back, "you gender-normative idiots."

All of them were brittle and terrified, as if clinging to banter kept the horror at bay.

Something inside me, something worse than hunger, woke.

I turned from the lab. Their voices faded but stayed inside me, a loop I couldn't switch off. What was I now? Ghost, monster, or witness? For the first time since the bite, I tried to shape a plan.

Hold my breath. Stay invisible.

Without a sound, the map in my head unfurled with perfect clarity.

Follow the hunger.

My stomach tightened, but it wasn't food I wanted. It was him. His voice. His laugh. His *lies*. My hunger had a name now, and it was Greg Beauchamp.

The school turned fuzzy around me, blotches of carnage, cracked windows, bodies in prom wear, but none of it mattered to me. Not anymore. I passed two more zombies chewing silently on what might've been a leg. They didn't look up, and I didn't stop. A trampled tiara glinted on the floor. At least someone made it to Prom Queen, however briefly. I stepped over a girl sobbing into her knees, somehow still human, somehow untouched. Circling her, I moved as if she were a patch of spilled water. I was beyond detours. There was only one destination.

Outside, Greg's scent hit me like a punch. His familiar cocktail of cologne, skin serum, and boyhood arrogance. I stood, breathing it in as if it could bring back the last few hours and make it all happen differently.

What it brought back was the car. The heat of his thigh against mine, the moment I leaned in, the windows dropping, and—

"Did you actually think I wanted to kiss you?"

My shoulder was knitting itself together, but inside, something kept tearing wider. His words were the only thing I couldn't heal from.

Under all of that, the echo of the whispers in the lab. Greg had left them when could have got a few in his car.

Full, ravenous hunger bloomed in my gut, but I doubted it was the mindless craving of the others. This wasn't about likes, reposts, or even survival, but focus. Purpose. I didn't want to find Greg; I wanted to consume him. I wanted him inside me, literally, because only then could I finish what he started.

CHAPTER SEVEN
THE TASTE OF TRUTH

AS I MADE my way towards the gym, I took one look back at the hall. Where it had once pulsed with colour, now it was just a block of stained brick and death and… *un*death.

The gym was different. Judging by the scarred brick on one corner, and the wrecked black Range Rover firmly embedded in the hedging opposite, Greg must have clipped the building, spun out, then made a run for it.

And there was Holly, front and centre of the crowd of zombies pressed against the gym's main doors murmuring in low, impatient growls. Their palms slid across the glass, like snails on a windowpane.

Greg must have made it inside then locked the doors behind him. I caught a glimpse of him through a narrow window, hair mussed, his tight shirt wet with what I guessed was sweat.

He's still beautiful.

Holding my breath, I joined the edges of the zombie horde, pressing one hand to the scarred brick wall, not to steady myself, but to feel something real before I walked into whatever came next.

The gym held many depressing memories of not being able to face soft tennis. Whenever I could, I'd—

Sneak out the back door.

Slowly, I made my way to the rear of the building and then took a lungful of air. And there it was—the back door, half hidden behind the bins. An invitation none of the others had remembered was there.

It can't be this easy, can it?

I gave the door a tug, but it wouldn't budge.

Guess not.

I'd always assumed I had a pretty good grip strength because, you know, *teenage boys*, but it was clear this door was going to need more than a couple of tugs to finish it off.

TMI?

Just as I made to give the door another pull, Holly rounded the corner, her hair matted, her lips parted slightly, and dark sludge leaking from the corner of her mouth. Her skin had the same blue tinge I'd seen in the mirror, but her eyes…

… her eyes were on me.

She looked, I looked back, and something passed between us. A flicker of what we were before?

I held my breath. Holly looked from left to right as though trying to make sense of my sudden absence, then she shuffled off, back from where she'd come.

As soon as I dared, I yanked the door again, and it opened just enough for me to slip through.

Greg stood alone in the centre of the space, surrounded by an improvised barricade of balance beams, chairs, and crash mats. A bunker built of fitness detritus. He turned when I entered, his eyes meeting mine.

No laughter this time. Recognition, yes, and a healthy dose of fear.

We stared at each other, and the silence practically hummed like something waiting to short-circuit.

He shifted behind his barricade, one hand gripping a chair leg like he might do something if I lunged. The other held his side, badly bandaged, blood seeping through the dressing. "I thought you were—"

"Dead?"

"Guess not." His hair hung lank, and his eyes were rimmed red. Fatigue, perhaps. Or crying. Both? "You're not like them, are you?" he said. "The others."

I didn't move. "I never was."

"I didn't mean for it to go like that. You know, in the car." He rubbed his face, smearing blood across his cheeks. "I gave the footie lads my spare key fob. Thought it'd be a laugh, part of the joke. I should've told them no, but when the windows went down and everyone was watching…" His voice cracked. "I laughed because that's what they expected." He swallowed hard. "But it wasn't a joke. Not really. I… I wanted it. I just didn't expect to want it that much.

And when they saw… When you saw…" His shoulders hunched like the words weighed more than he did. "I saw their faces, and I saw yours, and it scared the shit out of me."

I tilted my head. "Really?"

His voice dropped, cautious. "I didn't know what to do. Not around them." Looking away briefly, it seemed like the moment in the car had come back to him. "Thought they might just laugh it off."

"Oh, they laughed all right. And you along with them."

"I messed it up. All of it. I was scared and stupid, and I thought… I thought I could control it." His back met the barricade, and he winced, legs splayed, shoulders sagging. He looked at me like he was waiting for a verdict, but I wasn't there to judge. "I laughed because I thought I had to." His mouth twitched, as if he couldn't decide whether to apologise or spit.

The silence dragged, thick as mud, between us. He waited, eyes flicking and his hands restless. Every instinct in him must have been screaming for a reaction from me. A nod. Another word. Anything.

I gave him nothing.

His mouth suddenly curled. It didn't feel like cruelty but fear disguised as contempt. "Oh, come on," he spat. "You're not seriously going to do the whole strong, silent thing now?"

There was an absurd pleasure in watching his facade drop. Inside he was a scared little kid just like the rest of us.

He straightened, with a hint of his swagger returning. "Fine. Play the monster. That's all you ever were, really. Just needed the right excuse, didn't you?" He stepped out from behind the chairs. "You want me to say it? That I'm sorry? That I meant it? That I loved you?"

Did he mean it, or was he spitting out the word like it was poison? Did he want me to interrupt? To cut through the shame and tell him it wasn't too late?

Then he was on the approach, his voice tight with what seemed like angry frustration. "I don't get to be that person, okay?" He turned, fists clenched. "You looked at me like I could be someone else, someone like you, and I hated you for that, because I wanted to be someone else too, and... And you..." He took one more step, like he was challenging fate itself. "You were just the easiest way to find out."

He said it like a weapon or a curse, the last thing he had to throw at me before the truth came up and swallowed him.

I took a step forward. "Careful."

He flinched.

Another step.

He turned and ran, but not fast and not far. *He's lost too much blood.* He barely made it three metres before I reached him.

I didn't lunge, didn't roar, didn't drag him to the floor like an animal. I caught him by the arm, then pushed him down onto his back, straddling him, knees on either side of his ribs.

He thrashed once, breath hitching, eyes wide. "Jack," he whispered. "Please."

"The only thing I want," I said, voice low, "is what you couldn't say in the car."

Eyes clamped shut, he shook his head. "I want to, but—but I can't."

He didn't scream when I leaned in.

I could have stopped. Could have walked away, left him bleeding, left him alive. For a heartbeat, I imagined it: forgiving him, sparing him, pretending we were still two boys in a car before the windows dropped. Then I remembered the way he'd let me drown, and the moment evaporated.

My fingers threaded through his hair, gripping tight, as my face lowered to his. He was gloriously warm, and his lips parted like he thought I might kiss him. Maybe I wanted to. Maybe I almost did. My hand slid to the side of his face, thumb brushing the sweat from his temple. I held him like someone you mourn before the death. Then I opened my mouth and bit. Not savagely like the others but with rising pressure. Teeth to skin, then teeth to skull, then... through.

There's a sound brains make when you bite into them. It's soft and wet and it *sings*. The first hit was a jolt. A flash—Greg's eyes finding me across a classroom. Then another, clearer—the sound of his too-loud laugh stretched thin with fear. The memories came faster after that, tumbling over me until I couldn't tell which were mine and which were...

... *his?*

I saw myself through his eyes as he watched me across classroom after classroom, his gaze flickering away when he thought someone might see. I felt the clench of his jaw as he smiled too wide with friends after they'd mocked me behind my back. I heard his breath in the locker room stuttering as I walked past, pretending not to look. I felt panic in the car. The heat of it. The truth buried beneath the prank. He really liked me, but he hated the part of himself that reached out, and so he punished me for reaching back.

I saw all of it. Every lie, every fear, every swallowed word and twisted feeling, and when I was done, when the last taste of him dissolved on my tongue, I sat back.

His eyes stared past me, empty.

I touched my lips. Not with triumph, but quietly. I was full of him, of everything. And yet there was fullness without flavour, like finishing a meal you'd spent years craving, only to realise it wasn't what you wanted.

Shadows moved across the floor as the clouds shifted above the skylight, dark against the moon. They crept across the basketball court lines as if reclaiming the room.

The heavy aftertaste of him still coated my tongue. The memories kept coming, unfolding with such specificity it surprised me. I wasn't just recalling Greg; I was *hearing* him. His voice came from nowhere and everywhere.

"You can't say that out loud. Not here. Not with them."

"He looked at me again. Jesus, why does he keep—?"

An image followed. Me laughing with Holly outside the common room. Greg across the corridor, pretending to scroll through his phone, pretending not to glance up every five seconds.

I shook my head, trying to clear it, but more came.

"He makes it look so easy."

"He looks at me like he knows."

Suddenly I saw Greg in the bathroom, head bowed over a sink, punching the tap when the water scalded, and mumbling to his reflection.

"Get a grip."

The memories didn't just tell me who he was. They told me how hard he'd fought *not* to be who he was and how deeply he'd failed. He'd never let anyone in until I cracked his skull open and let him pour through me.

The echoes kept coming. Not just moments, but mood, tone, and texture. The stutter in his breath when I'd laugh, the thrill when he spoke to me, the shame that followed like a hangover.

"I'm not like him."

"I can't be like him."

"Maybe I'm just curious."

It excused nothing. The humiliation or the cruelty.

His body lay under me, slack and still, and I wasn't sure who I pitied more. Me or the boy who could never let himself want something honest.

The gym felt smaller now. Not like it had shrunk, more like I'd grown too large for it. Too heavy with everything I'd taken in. Greg's memories still swirled in my skull, not sharp but present, and I didn't try to shut them out.

I walked away, through the back door, away from the school, and out into the unknown.

I was done waiting to be chosen.

CHAPTER EIGHT
THE SIGNAL

OUT IN THE STREET, in the hush of the early hours, the air was still. Nothing moved. Not the trees and not the clouds.

Behind me, the school was a tomb.

Puddles caught glimmers of that strange peach-pink sky that comes just before dawn, but everything felt... *off*. The silence before a scream.

In another world, Greg and I might have been boyfriends. We could have lived in our own little parallel series of *Heartstopper* except our hearts had actually stopped.

The part of me that had wanted him, hated him, needed him... all of it was empty now, and the emptiness was worse than hunger.

I closed my eyes, tried to listen to Greg's thoughts, but they'd slipped away.

Wait. Has my heart stopped?

I could hold my breath to stay invisible, but that meant I usually needed to breathe, which meant oxygen was getting into my bloodstream, which meant...

I pressed my hand to my chest, and there it was. A heartbeat.

Then, the moment snapped. That sharp screeching cut through the quiet, punching through my skull like a migraine made of thumb tacks.

That sound. It's doing something.

Yes, that was it. First, the Missy Elliott song and the prickling in my forearms, then Carmen DeVyre's song and that terrible sound. And the cabbage soup had vibrated like it heard it. Holly had laced it with Carmen's additive, so was that a conductor? A trigger? Is that why I hadn't turned? Had the soup clinging to my arms when I'd washed up Holly's Stanley cup given me some sort of resistance?

I started walking, slowly at first, then faster.

The streets were empty, but fear walked beside me, whispering that I should go home, but—

Should I?

I wanted to go home. Really. To find Mum in her chair with her chips and her sarcasm.

"If I were you, I'd stay home and watch telly. Less risk of being emotionally eviscerated."

She'd been right. And that was exactly why I couldn't go back.

I've been eviscerated.

If I went home, by the time I got there, whatever it was that turned me this far might have taken hold. I couldn't trust what I'd do, couldn't let her see me like this. If she opened the door, I didn't know whether I'd hug her or bite her, and if it was the second one, I'd never forgive myself. Better she wondered where I'd gone than risk being the monster on her doorstep.

And the sound was still out there, still... calling. If I didn't try to stop it, more people would turn. I had to follow it, had to understand what I was becoming before it decided for me.

At the corner of Romero Street, a boy hunched at the bus stop, head in his hands. His tux was surprisingly intact, but blood crusted the collar of his shirt, and his hands shook like a tremor was deep in his bones.

He looked up slowly, eyes a little cloudy, but not gone.

Amit?

He straightened when he saw me, like he might bolt.

"Don't," I said, stopping a few feet away. "I'm not —" I almost said *dangerous*, but I wasn't sure that was true.

"You're like me," he whispered. "You didn't turn all the way."

I nodded. "Yeah."

His voice rose. "I thought I was the only one."

"Me too."

"I went home," he said quietly. "My mum and my little sister... they were already gone. Eyes like ice. They came at me as if I were dinner. I locked the door and ran."

"You have to hold your breath. It's like they can't see you if you hold your breath."

"Oh." His gaze fell to the floor.

"I'm sorry," I said, and I meant it.

He nodded, eyes shining. "I wanted to help them, but what could I do? I don't even know what I am anymore."

"We're something in between."

He wiped at his nose, then gave me another look. Quieter this time. "You're weirdly calm about all this."

Maybe I was. Maybe the soup was hollowing me out, leaving me calm because there was nothing left to burn.

"I've had a long night."

Amit huffed a tired laugh. When he looked at me again, something unfamiliar—a flicker of warmth that wasn't hunger or rage—settled somewhere behind my ribs.

"There's a signal," I said, glancing toward the horizon. "I mean, I think there's a signal. It's got something to do with all this."

"I heard it," he murmured. "Like something was crawling behind my eyes. I just thought it was part of —" He gestured between us. "—that awful music."

"I think it triggered the changes somehow. Holly started with her gran's cabbage soup, but it was some TikToker's additive that gave the signal something to work with."

"Like the soup's the software, and the signal's the install command?"

"Maybe." I paused. "Who bit you?"

"No one," he said with a blank expression.

"Wait… You drank the soup?"

He shrugged. "I wanted to lose weight."

"But there's nothing of you."

He studied me, his gaze stuck to mine, then a ghost of a smile pulled at his mouth, revealing a chipped tooth and dimples. "Because I drank the soup."

Idiot.

"Oh," I said. "Right. So why didn't you change? Everyone who drank the soup changed completely. I just assumed I didn't because I'd only been bitten."

Amit narrowed his eyes. "You didn't drink the soup?"

"No, I've got more self-respect than to…"

He grimaced.

Shit. "Sorry."

"Forget it," he said with a shrug. "What are you going to do?"

"I don't know," I said. "Find it, I guess. Figure out how to stop it."

He stood, wincing slightly as he adjusted his weight. When he looked at me again, there was something steadier behind his eyes. "I'm coming with you."

"No, you don't have to."

"Look," he said, shifting again. "I don't want to be alone."

Two half-broken boys against whatever this was.

It didn't sound like much, but maybe it was enough to start with.

I gave him my most reassuring smile. "You're not alone. Not now."

We walked together into the quiet street, and even though the world was ending, a part of me stayed focused on the way our steps matched up, just slightly. And under the rhythm of our footsteps, I could still hear the signal, low and insistent, waiting for us to follow.

ACKNOWLEDGMENTS

This story wouldn't exist without Erin Michelle's Short Story Summer. Thank you, Erin, for believing in what was then called *No Brainer*. The brief was 4,000 words, but I simply couldn't stop writing...

Huge thanks to my beta readers Emily Klitou, Margaret McNellis, Hannah Kelley, and Cate Townsend who braved the brain-munching, cabbage-fuelled chaos of this book and still had the kindness to point out where it could be even better. Your feedback was sharp, generous, and often exactly what I didn't know I needed. This story wouldn't be half as alive (or half as undead) without you.

ABOUT THE AUTHOR

Stuart is an author and book coach who writes about men who love men. He has been published by Dreamspinner Press and Vine Leaves Press, and his latest book, *Behind the Seams*, was a BookLife Prize Fiction Contest Semifinalist.

Stuart holds an MA in Professional Writing and lives in the UK with his husband, pets and too many Ken dolls for a man his age.

ALSO BY STUART WAKEFIELD

BEHIND THE SEAMS

A 2021 BookLife Prize Fiction Contest Semifinalist!

Praise for *Behind the Seams*:

"Sumptuous detailed descriptions of clothing and the art of sewing and fashion design are what make this story a cut above other gay romances. Wakefield develops the relationship between Kit and Barker in tandem with the filming of the episodes of a reality TV show and that device adds interest and tension to the story." — The 2021 BookLife Prize Fiction Contest Critic's Report

"A heart-warming gay romance in a fresh and vivid setting."

"Excellent telling of a classic human story set in one of the more bonkers corners of our modern world."

"Everything was good: the characters, the pacing, the conflicts, the humour, the banter, all of it."

When apprentice Savile Row tailor Kit Redman auditions for smash-hit UK TV show Runway Rivals, he's instantly drawn to charismatic fellow auditionee Barker Wareham.

After a disastrous audition at the hands of savage fashion editor, and Runway Rivals judge, Nancy Shearsmith, Kit's convinced he won't get through, but he's wrong.

As filming begins, Kit comes face-to-face with Barker, who makes it clear it's all about winning the show and nothing more.

But there's more to Barker than meets the eye.

Now, with Nancy intent on ruining Kit's dream of becoming a world-class fashion designer, can he ever hope to win the show and get the man?

OUT IN THE COLD

Step back in time to 1887 Montana, a land brimming with untamed beauty and the harsh realities of a brutal winter known as the 'Big Die-Up'. Out in the Cold is a gripping romance that intertwines the lives of Faron Noble, a resilient ranch hand, and Marius Tillman, his enigmatic boss.

Amidst a devastating winter that threatens their very livelihood, Faron and Marius battle not only the elements but also their burgeoning feelings for each other in a world unprepared for their love.

Faron, with his unwavering strength and quiet determination, navigates the perils of ranch life and the complexities of his heart. Marius, a man of the land, yet a stranger to the affairs of the heart, finds in Faron a warmth that the cold Montana winter cannot freeze.

Out in the Cold is more than just a love story; it is a journey of self-discovery, resilience, and the courage to embrace one's true self in the face of adversity. This novel will take you on an emotional rollercoaster, through the struggles and triumphs of Faron and Marius, as they confront injury, a merciless winter, and the societal constraints of their time.

Perfect for fans of historical romance and poignant love stories like *Brokeback Mountain*, Out in the Cold offers an intimate glimpse into the lives of two men who dare to defy the norms, united by love and a shared fight for survival against the odds.

BODY OF WATER

A #1 Gay Fiction Best Seller, Body of Water, is the first novel in The Orcadian, and 1 of 10 books long-listed for the Polari First Book Prize for a first book which explores the LGBT experience:

"Fear the water."

Leven has never forgotten his mother's terrible warning. So how can he explain his strange attraction to water, his powerful sensitivity to it, his extraordinary ability to swim as though possessed?

Water is Leven's natural element.

And it's water that takes the one he loves and destroys everything he's ever called his own.

Set on the Orkney Islands in the mysterious realm of Selkie mythology, Leven's story of lost identity, lost love, and the search for redemption leads him from London to a terrifying meeting with the dark and volatile man who will change his heart forever.

Something in the water is coming for Leven.

But can a man born of chaos ever calm the storm?

MEMORY OF WATER

Despondent and suicidal over the disappearance of his beloved Leven, Shaun goes from medical observation to the River Thames—where he wades into the freezing water intent upon ending it all.

Instead, Shaun finds himself rescuing the mysterious floating body of a man in strange armour. And he learns that Leven is not dead, hope is not lost, love is not over. . .and the world of London is not the world he thought it was at all.

Shaun and his sister Beth struggle to save the life of this man so like Leven as to be identical, although he has no memory of Shaun or anything that's happened to him.

When their struggle becomes one of escaping their own tyrannical parents and violent past, it is Beth's wild, uncontrollable art that brings to them the clues Shaun needs to piece together where Leven has been, what happened to him there, who's coming for him now. . .and how only a fine thread of precognition hangs between London and oceanic apocalypse.

Before it's too late, Shaun must recover this man's memory — The memory of water.

GOODMAN'S CHILD

Praise for Goodman's Child:

"It's beautifully written and observed on many different levels - from the descriptions of the Orkney landscape, to Moire's emotions, to making

folklore a reality - it just flows and I love it!" – Kate
Tenbeth, author of Burly & Grum and Unlucky Dip.

"…a thoughtful, beautifully written tale that evokes
Kafka's 'Metamorphosis' or, perhaps more closely,
Roger McGough's wonderful poem 'Angel Wings'"
– Mark Watkins, co-author of Keeping Mum.

"Moire stood in the croft house's porch, watching
Goodman leave, plotting her escape. His boots crunched in
the shoal of pebbles he'd salvaged from the shore behind
the house and its many outbuildings.

She'd long since given up wondering what lay beyond the
dry stone wall that marked the perimeter of her
understanding because, once lured there by Goodman,
she'd never been able to leave. Besides, her thoughts ever
returned to the weight of the sea and of freedom she hadn't
known in seven years."